the LiTTLEST
inventor

Written by Mandi C. Mathis   Illustrated by Danielle Ragogna

The Littlest Inventor

All marketing and publishing rights guaranteed to and reserved by:

721 W. Abram St., Arlington, TX 76013

Phone: 817.277.0727

Toll free: 800.489.0727

Fax: 817.277.2270

Online: www.SensoryWorld.com

Email: info@sensoryworld.com

© 2016 Mandi C. Mathis

Illustrated by Danielle Ragogna

ISBN: 9781935567622

— *Dedication* —

Kalie, Tyson & Sawyer

*You light up my life
like a Tesla coil.*

The littlest inventor went to the store.

It was crowded and loud, the shopping a bore.

The noises too loud, the lights too bright.

I started to feel nervous, fight or flight.

When I realized I couldn't handle the tension.
I decided ... Hey! I'll make an invention.

This shouldn't be so hard, there's got to be a way
to overcome what I'm feeling here today.

I even started to feel somewhat sickly.
I plugged my ears with my hands and got home quickly.

Up the stairs to my room, I slam my door.
My family has no idea what's in store.

So I started working just as quickly as I could,

and knew what I had decided would be really good.

I emerged with a contraption!
My family didn't know what was about to happen.

So back to the store we went in a hurry,
fingers crossed, and minds full of worry.

We got out of the car and walked to the door.

Gingerly our feet touched the smooth floor.

I suited up and said, "Here goes ..."

and had a new look from my head to my toes.

A hat made with headphones, a
weighted vest under my lab coat,

and even chewy dog tags hung
loose around my throat.

Fidget in my hands, heavy boots on my feet, I knew I had
to buy something to eat.

My cologne was strong just how I like it.
I started to shop, no crying nor fit.

As I completed shopping for everything I needed,

my family just really couldn't believe it.

GOGGLE-HEADPHONES TO BLOCK LOUD NOISES AND BRIGHT LIGHTS.

CHEWY DOG TAGS IN CASE OF ANTSINESS.

FAVORITE COLOGNE WITH A PLEASANT SCENT.

WEIGHTED VEST FOR AN EXTRA-CALMING HUG.

FIDGETS FOR FOCUSING.

HEAVY BOOTS FOR GREATER COMFORT.

In my new uniform—sensory superhero meets littlest inventor!

I finally conquered the shopping center!

CPSIA information can be obtained
at www.ICGtesting.com
Printed in the USA
BVOW10s1202270516

449743BV00001B/1/P

9 781935 567622